Let's Fast Forward to the Good Stuff

ISBN: 978-1-949265-03-3 (Paperback)
ISBN: 978-1-949265-02-6 (Ebook)

Library of Congress Control Number: 2019915905

Printed in the United States of America

Business inquiries: getchrissynow@gmail.com

www.getchrissy.com

CONTENTS

"Where is the fast-forward button? Let's fast forward to the good stuff!"

CHAPTER ONE

The Kooky Drifter

IT WAS a chilly morning. The city was covered in an icy fog, blurring the streets. Ross looked out the window, picturing days like this with his father. In those days, there was no such thing as making his father wait. Ross could recall his father throwing a can of soda, or one of his favorite cans of soup against the living room wall, screaming, "What's taking you so long, boy? You're making me wait longer than I have to! I'm coming up there to get you, right now!"

He remembered those days with his father far too well.

Ross walked over to the sofa in his living room, drinking out of a can of soda. When he finished, he put his nose up to the opening of the can and sniffed inside. Then he crushed the can in his hand and flung it across the room.

Ross lay down on the sofa, grabbed his foot, and peeled off a nail from one of his toes. He put the toenail in his mouth and chewed it while his eyes glanced over at a small rubber ball on the floor. He reached for the ball and tossed it against the wall. It was almost time for him to get dressed for work, and his best friend, Glen, was sitting on the recliner chair near him, reading the sports section of the newspaper.

"Can time go any slower?" Ross said. "That clock just sits on the wall there, taking its sweet old time."

Glen didn't even look up when the ball bounced off the wall.

"Why does everything have to go so slow in life?" Ross said. "I get so tired of waiting around. Where is the fast-forward button?"

Glen rose from his seat and walked to the clock. Ross tossed the ball again and Glen snatched it out of the air. "If you could zoom past everything, where would the fun be in that?"

"A lot of fun!" Ross sat upright on the sofa. "Let's fast forward to the good stuff."

"Let me guess. You still think you're going to strike it rich?" Glen asked.

"You're right about that one!" Ross pulled out a handful of lottery tickets from his pockets. "I know it's going to happen soon."

"I got some bad news for you."

"What?"

"It's never going to happen." Glen placed the rubber ball on the coffee table in front of the sofa and felt his pockets for his keys.

"I have to head out for work. Don't forget about our trip to the playoff game this weekend," Glen said.

"Don't worry," Ross said, "I'll be ready!"

Glen grabbed his things and walked out the door.

*****

The next evening, Ross stayed at work later than usual. When he left, he was caught in heavy traffic, and not one car was moving.

Ross put his car in park and stuck his head out the window, honking his horn. "Hurry up! I'm trying to get to the store!"

"Hey, what's your problem? It's probably an accident up the road!" a man driving a small convertible yelled.

Ross pointed at the driver and laughed. "I hope that's your girlfriend's car, buddy!"

"How about you mind your own beeswax?" the driver yelled back.

Ross put one leg out the car window while holding the roof handle on the car ceiling, leaning his body on top of the window seal, shouting, "Who did it? Which one of you geniuses caused an accident?"

Many of the drivers looked at him, frightened, and rolled up their windows.

"You're looking for the folks up the road! Not us!" a driver in a red car said.

"Get back in your car and wait like the rest of us!" a trucker shouted.

After about thirty minutes or so, and several shouting matches later, the lanes began to move. Ross tucked his body back into his car, hoping he could still make it to the store. When traffic got lighter, he zoomed through the streets, switching lanes as fast as he could.

Ross arrived at the store and walked inside; It was packed. He grabbed a bag of chips, a couple of cans of soup, and a can of soda. By the time he finished, the checkout lane stretched down the aisle.

Ross stood behind the long line. "Can someone open another check stand around here?"

The cashier looked at him but said nothing.

"Hellooooooooo!" Ross stomped his feet hard on the ground.

The cashier still did not say a word.

Ross darted his eyes at the cashier. His thoughts raced. His heart pounded hard in his chest. He squeezed the bag of chips in his hand until it popped. Then, he threw his groceries on one of the shelves in the aisle.

Ross approached the register, shoving the customer's shopping carts out of his way. He climbed on top of the check stand and walked down the conveyor belt.

"Hey, get off my grits!" an older customer yelled.

"He's crushing my zucchini!" another customer said.

Ross got to the register—bent over with his hands on his knees— staring down the cashier. He threw one of his arms behind him, pointing at the customers who were in line. "Don't you see all these people waiting?"

"Sir, please get off the check stand," the cashier said.

"Open another register, now!"

"We are short-handed tonight."

"Go get the manager!"

"Sir, I'm the store manager." The cashier pointed to the badge on his shirt.

"You have got to be kidding me!" Ross leaped over the register into a pile of bagged groceries. He pushed one of the store clerks out of his way while hopping down from the check stand.

Then he marched out of the store.

There was too much waiting around, and too many delays in life. It seemed like everyone and everything wanted to slow him down. He decided he would just go home.

*****

Ross raced down the street in his car. When the light turned red, he slammed his foot on the break. He slugged the steering wheel with his fist. "I just missed it!"

He started to run the red light but saw a woman standing on the sidewalk with a small boy and girl. Ross watched them shiver in their jackets, waiting at the bus stop. The girl hugged her mother by the waist, and the boy rubbed his hands together to stay warm.

Ross pulled over to the side of the road and approached them. "It's a little chilly out here, don't you think? You guys are starting to look like popsicles!"

"We can't move into our new place for a couple of days," the woman said. "We're going to take a bus up north to my mothers."

Ross laughed. "That bus ride alone is going to take about two days."

"We don't have much of a choice," the woman said.

"If you trust me, I can take you guys to a motel."

The woman shook her head. "Thank you, but—"

"Don't worry." Ross took out his wallet and opened it. "I can read your mind from here."

"Sir, I couldn't take your—"

"Get these kids out of the cold!" Ross put some money in her hand. "Call a cab and get a room for a couple nights."

"Thank you so much!" the woman said.

"No problem." Ross ran to his car and flew home.

*****

The next few days crawled by. Ross saw a package in front of his door, and red spots sprinkled along his porch.

Weird. I didn't order anything.

He picked up the package but noticed there wasn't a shipping address or return label. In the past, his neighbor Harvey's packages had been mistakenly dropped off on his porch.

Ross walked to Harvey's house, and knocked on the door, but no one answered. After he knocked a second time, he heard a car pulling up behind him.

Harvey parked his pickup truck in the driveway and got out. "Hey, Ross. Is that a gift for me?"

"Maybe. Is this yours?" Ross walked over to him with the package.

Harvey looked at the box. "Nope, that ain't mine! But I saw the person who left it."

"Who was it?"

"Some kooky drifter."

"Really?"

"Yup. I saw her hanging outside your home. She tried opening your door and then looked through the windows. That's when I decided to walk up to her. When I got closer, I saw that she wore a purple veil that covered her face, and her clothes were shredded into pieces."

Ross scratched his head. "That doesn't sound like one of my girlfriends."

"I reckon it wasn't. Because when she moved the veil to scratch herself, her skin was hanging all off her face. Her nose and mouth were all twisted out of shape, drooping over to one side. I ain't never seen a face like that before."

"What the…" Ross said.

"You ain't heard nothing yet. After I told her you weren't home, and put the package down on your porch, she pitched a big, ole, hissy fit. She started arguing with herself and placed the package down in front of your door. Out of nowhere, she laughed out of control. I tell ya, she was having a good ole laugh with herself. I'm guessing she was drooling blood because when she laughed, something red was dripping from under her veil."

Ross's eyes got wider. "She leaked on my porch?"

"Yup, and at that point, I walked away to call the police, looking over my shoulder to make sure she wasn't following me. When I opened my front door, I looked back, but she had run off."

Ross felt a heavy feeling in his stomach. "For once in my life, I'm glad I was at work."

"Yea, it was weird and—"

"Did you call the police?"

"Nope."

"Why not?"

"Because she left."

"Hmm, she ran off, huh?"

"I figured she got scared and skedaddled."

Ross shook the package in his hands "I wonder who it could have been?!"

"Probably just someone playing a trick on ya. Don't think too much of it."

"Maybe you're right," Ross said. "Thanks for your help."

Ross went back to his home, searching outside to see if the woman had left anything else. When he walked inside, he placed the package on top of his kitchen counter and grabbed his cleaning supplies from the hall closet.

He couldn't help but think about the mysterious woman who had left the package. Maybe, it was the Siren of Pisces?

Ross had always been obsessed with Greek mythology, and among all its legends, none fascinated him more than the Sirens of the Sea—especially the elusive Siren of Pisces.

Maybe she delivered the package, he thought.

According to the stories he had collected over the years, the Siren of Pisces was one of the most beautiful mythical beings ever spoken of. She walked among ordinary people disguised as a beautiful woman whose face was hidden behind a lavender veil. It was said that whenever she laughed, the blood of the chaotic souls she had already claimed leaked from the corners of her mouth. A reminder of those who had accepted her gift, only to be consumed by the darkness within themselves.

The old tales claimed she appeared only when a person's life stood at a crossroads. Some believed she came to those consumed by chaos; others claim she sought out the kind-hearted and genuinely selfless. She never arrived without purpose.

She carried gifts that promised to fulfill a person's deepest desire. But every gift demanded a price. For some, it became a blessing or a reward for the goodness they had shown the world. For others, it was merely bait, luring them deeper into the very chaos that lived within them.

Ross couldn't help but wonder if the package waiting for him had come from her.

It couldn't be. Ross thought. "*There's no way!*"

Ross went to the porch and poured the cleaning mix where he saw the red spots. He let the mix soak in for a second and then rinsed the porch down with the garden hose. When he was done, he put the supplies back into the closet and walked into the kitchen to get a can of soda out the fridge. When Ross turned around, a small note lay on top of the package.

It had not been there before.

He jumped up, spilling the soda all over the counter.

Am I losing it, or what?

Ross grabbed the note. Under his breath he whispered, "Use what is in this box to fast forward to your place of choice within your thoughts. Use only once. If not..."

The soda had smeared the last of the words.

This had to be one of Glen's pranks. Ross shook his head. He put the note on top of the fridge and took a small towel from his kitchen drawer to clean the spill. Once the counter was cleaned, Ross pounced on his sofa to watch TV but soon fell asleep.

*****

The next morning, Ross awoke to the sound of his neighbor's lawn mower blasting through his window. Ross looked up at his alarm clock that he forgot to set.

He was late for work.

Ross arrived at work and rushed to his office, passing by his coworkers.

"Ross has one foot out the door," one of them said.

"His days are numbered," another said.

Ross snuck past his boss's office.

"You're late!" Tank growled.

Ross walked back and stood in Tank's doorway. "Yeah. Traffic was a nightmare."

Tank got up from his chair, walking to the espresso machine in his office, and poured himself a cup of coffee. His eyes were sealed on Ross, slowly sipping from his mug.

Ross's hand sweated on the handle of his leather bag. His muscles tense all over.

Tank took another sip of his coffee, staring at him.

Ross's pulse was racing.

"Tank!" someone yelled. "You got a sec?"

"Yea. I'm coming," Tank said.

Ross moved away from the door as Tank left his office.

"Man, that was a close one!" Ross said.

*****

Early the next day, Ross called off sick from work. He and Glen decided to leave a day earlier for the playoff game that weekend.

Ross was packing his clothes when he heard the phone ring. "Hello."

"Hey, best bud, it's Glen. Are you almost ready?"

"I'm still packing up my things. Oh, and I got your little package."

"What package?"

"This is the lamest joke ever!"

"What are you talking about, Ross?"

"Your lame pranks!"

"I still don't have any clue what you're talking about. I'll be over there soon."

"Whatever you say." Ross hung up the phone.

An hour later, Ross heard someone in his driveway honking the horn. Ross looked out the window and saw Glen getting out of his car. He walked over to unlock the front door and dragged his luggage against the wall.

Afterwards, he went into his bedroom to make sure he hadn't forgotten something. Within a few minutes, he left his room to find Glen next to the kitchen counter.

Glen pointed at the box on the counter. "Is this the package you're accusing me of?"

"You're the guilty party!" Ross said. "Remember our little talk the other day?"

"About how you want to zoom through life?" Glen said.

"Isn't it funny that this package was dropped off with a note talking about that very thing?" Ross grabbed the note from on top of the fridge.

"Are you serious?"

Ross waived the note in Glen's face. "Very serious!"

Glen pushed back Ross's hand. "You think I would go through the trouble?"

"Yes, I do!" Ross said. "I'm pretty sure you had on one of your old Halloween costumes."

"Ross, I—"

"This is just like when you tore those stupid pictures out of that magazine and stuck them on the passenger side of my car in college," Ross said.

"That was a million years ago." Glen chuckled.

"Everyone was honking at me that day and giving me crazy looks!"

"Ross, I didn't write this note, nor did I bring that package here."

"Maybe, it wasn't you." Ross took a sharp blade from the kitchen drawer. "Did you put Charlotte up to this?"

Glen looked at the blade in Ross's hand. "No, I didn't. We both know my wife is not very fond of you, now, don't we?"

"True." Ross said. "Charlotte has never liked me."

"What do you plan on doing with that blade?" Glen asked.

"I want to see what's inside this mystery box," Ross said.

Ross placed the package on top of the dining room table and sat down on one of the dining room chairs. Glen took a seat right in front of him. They both sat there and didn't move a muscle.

"Then that only means one thing," Ross said.

"What?

"She did it."

"Who?"

Ross pointed at his collection of Greek Mythology books on the floor.

"Oh, no!" Glen put his hands on his face, shaking his head. "Not this crap again."

"It's gotta be the Siren of—"

"No, it's not, you're nuts!" Glen said.

"What are you waiting for? "Glen pushed the blade closer to Ross. "Let's open it!"

"Don't you want to do it?" Ross scooted the blade to Glen.

"Nope." Glen moved the blade back to Ross.

"Fine!" Ross picked up the blade, slicing under the flaps on both sides of the top of the box. After cutting both sides, he lifted the box top with one hand and slowly cut down the middle.

The flaps on the box sprang open.

Ross and Glen looked inside.

It was a remote control.

The hand-held device had a fast-forward button, a rewind button, and a small light bulb at the very top.

"That's the mystery of the box?" Ross picked up the remote. "This is the grand finale?"

"I can't believe it!" Glen said.

Ross looked into Glen's eyes. "This is incredible."

Glen sighed. "We don't even know if this thing even works."

"I read that the Siren of Pisces can grant your desires."

"Did you read that from a fortune cookie?"

"No, I didn't!"

"Sounds like it," Glen yawned. "So, what exactly is that thing supposed to do?"

"Teleport us to any planet or gas station that we want."

"Huh?"

"In the note, it said we can zoom to any place in our minds." Ross got up and placed the blade back into the drawer.

"Oh man, creepy just got creepier," Glen said. "I'm not sure if I can make it to Mercury today."

"Wait, what?"

"Hurry up! We're already late for our trip."

"You don't even want to know what might happen?"

"No! This is just too weird," Glen said. "Especially, that whole thing about the strange woman coming here."

"This may be a real thing," Ross said. "If the remote is truly magical, then I can just zoom to any place in my head."

"You did say you were going to win the lottery," Glen said.

"Yes. I can feel it in my bones."

"When do you believe this miracle is going to happen?"

"I know it will happen within a few years."

Glen laughed. "Actually, I've had a sudden change of heart."

"Now you're on board with this?"

"I want you to teleport into the future." Glen chuckled. "And bring me back some of your lottery winnings."

"I know I'm going to win," Ross said. "That's what's ahead for me!"

"Sure, it is!" Glen put his hand on his face and laughed.

"Don't laugh too hard," Ross said. "You might end up coming with me."

"Before you lift off into space, I'll make sure to stand as far back as I can."

Glen stood out of his chair and walked down the hallway, passing the kitchen. He could see Ross from afar.

"Ok, here I go!" Ross rested his finger on the fast-forward button.

Glen laughed. "I want to see this magic trick where you turn into sparkling, little crystals and vanish into thin air!"

Ross stared at the remote in his hand.

"Will you get it over with already!" Glen shouted.

Ross held his breath and pushed fast forward.

CHAPTER TWO

Store Showdown

BETWEEN ONE blink and the next, Ross went from standing in his kitchen to standing in a small bedroom. The four walls of the room were painted blue.

A calendar featuring classic, souped-up cars and trucks hung in the center of one wall. There were action figures piled together in a corner in the closet. A football lay cozy on the pillows of the small bed, and an old radio mounted on top of the wooden dresser.

It was his old bedroom inside his parent's home.

Ross looked at Glen on the other side of the room.

"Are you Glen from the future?"

"No. It's still the same ole me that's on this silly ride with you," Glen said.

"You weren't even standing next to me," Ross said.

"I know," Glen said. "How did I get involved in your crazy time warp?"

"Maybe, because you opened the package with me," Ross said.

"Oh great!" Glen threw up his arms in the air. "We should sell this thing. It would make us a fortune." "We would swim in dough! "Ross said.

"Oh, wait. We can't sell it," Glen said. "Didn't the note say we couldn't go back?"

"The note said to use only once," Ross said.

"Well, that's it for that. I guess we're stuck."

"I cannot believe this!" Ross said.

"Things have gotten worse for you. This is hilarious!"

"Yea, laugh it up!" Ross walked to the calendar hanging on the wall. "That remote took us exactly three Years into the future."

"Right into your old bedroom at your parent's house." Glen said.

"I'm going back to where we were last," Ross said. "My lottery dream is never going to happen."

"I can see that!" Glen chuckled.

"Ross," his father called. "Do you have company up there?"

"There's no way I'm living with my parents again in this terrible town," Ross said.

Ross held up the remote in his hand.

"Do not touch any buttons!" Glen yelled.

"No way!"

"Let's just figure things out from here," Glen said. "It just may land us somewhere like on a volcano or Pluto."

"Only if we think about something silly like that," Ross said.

"Ross!" his father yelled.

Ross looked at Glen. "I'm not living here with my parents again. Especially, my dad."

Ross pressed the rewind button.

*****

When they blinked, they were back in Ross's home.

"Were back!" Glen said.

Ross looked at his luggage by the door. "Right where we were before we pushed the button."

Glen stared at the remote in Ross's hand. "What were you thinking about before you pressed the button each time?"

Ross grew quiet for a moment.

"I was thinking about three Years from now on the first go. The second go, I was thinking about returning to my home before we pushed the button."

"Bingo!" Glen grabbed the remote from Ross. "So, it is in fact powered by our minds."

"Just like the note said."

"This is incredible!" Glen said. "It's some old, weird time machine that allows us to go anywhere by using our thoughts."

"It's amazing!" Ross snatched the remote away from Glen. "It defies all logic in life."

Glen took a seat on the sofa. "How did it know whose thoughts to take on?"

"Maybe, since I was the one that pushed it, it tapped into my thoughts."

Glen laughed. "I'm glad it was your thoughts instead of mine."

"Why is that?"

"I was thinking about that volcano."

"Bathing in burning lava?" Ross said. "Sounds very relaxing."

"Well, we have another issue," Glen said.

"What now?"

"I'm not interested in coming along these time rollercoasters with you," Glen said.

"Huh?" Ross said.

"We need to figure out how far back I need to stand, so I don't have to get sucked into your next ride."

Ross set the remote on the coffee table. "Is that really your complaint here?"

"Pretty much," Glen said.

"We found a gold mine that will make us a bucket load of cash, defies all laws of logic of this universe, and your concern is that you don't want to be along for the ride?"

"I've been knowing you for far too long," Glen said. "Believe me when I say I'm not interested in going to any faraway places in your head!"

"I think there could be more secrets about this thing," Ross said. "Let's go somewhere else."

"Actually." Glen grabbed the remote. "I think it's my turn!"

"Just a second ago you said you didn't want anything to do with it," Ross said.

"You got it all wrong." Glen flipped around the small-time machine in his hands.

"What do I have wrong?"

"I don't want anything to do with your colorful imagination," Glen said. "However, I'm perfectly okay with my own."

"What does that even mean?"

"I don't want to be along on your ride, but I'm perfectly fine with my own."

"Be my guest," Ross said. "Where are we going?"

"Oh, you're not coming with me."

"Well, I don't think you have a choice," Ross said, "Because it places us with each other."

"Did you hear something?" Glen said.

"I thought I did."

Glen walked to the front window and pulled back the curtain. The pitch-black sky was cloudless and clear. The glow from the moon quietly crept into the room.

"You see anyone?" Ross said.

"Nope!" Glen looked down at his watch. "We're going to have to cancel our trip."

"I agree." Ross grabbed the remote from Glen.

"Let's fool around with it tomorrow," Glen said.

"Sure. It's getting late. We might as well see about it tomorrow," Ross said.

Glen walked to the front door. "Don't touch it until I get back tomorrow!"

"You got it!" Ross said.

Glen left outside to his car.

*****

Ross laid the remote on the coffee table. He walked to the front door and locked it.

Ross turned around. He gazed at the remote.

He walked into the kitchen and took a can of soda out of the fridge. On his way back to the sofa, he turned on the television.

Ross plopped down on the sofa with the soda can. His eyes were watching the remote.

Ross took a glance at the clock on the wall. It was getting later in the evening. He put the soda back in the fridge and walked into his bedroom to take a shower. When he was done, he put on his pajamas and leaped into bed.

Ross tossed and turned in his sheets. He jumped out of bed and walked to the bathroom sink and turned on the faucet. He threw water on his face and dried himself with his shirt.

Ross left out into the living room. His eyes studied the magical remote on the coffee table without blinking.

"I can't take it anymore!" Ross snatched the remote off the coffee table.

Where could I possibly go with it?

"The market!" Ross put the remote in his pocket.

He jumped into his car with the remote, speeding off to the small supermarket near his home. He drove up to the store and got out of his car and put the remote in his back pocket.

Ross walked into the supermarket and the lines were packed down the aisles, again. He noticed there were two cashiers this time, and remembered the other cashier being the manager of the store. He grabbed a few packs of soda and got in line.

"Here we go again!" Ross paced in and out of the line. "This place cannot get it together!"

Some of the customers remembered Ross from his last visit. They whispered amongst each other, giggling and pointing at him. The manager looked back to see where the ruckus was coming from, and recognized Ross in the line.

"Welcome back, sir," the manager said. "We would appreciate if you could stay off the check stand this time!"

Everyone laughed that heard the manager, but not Ross.

Ross slit his eyes and clenched his jaw. His chest tightened as his heart rate climbed at a tremendous speed. He threw his groceries on the floor. The packs of soda burst, splattering all over on those around him.

"Cleanup on aisle four!" a voice on the intercom said.

"You got that right!" Ross yelled.

A store clerk with a mop rushed over to clean up the mess. Ross grabbed the mop from him, pushing him away.

Everyone stood in silence, looking at Ross twirling the mop in his hand.

"Sir,"—the manager's voice trembled—"were going to have to ask you to leave."

"All I ask is for faster service!" Ross shouted. "Why is that so hard for you people?"

The store manager ran from the register to the phone in his office. Ross hurried behind him and ripped the phone cord from out of the wall. The store manager screamed in a high pitch voice as Ross chased him out of the store, waving the mop in his hand.

Ross came back inside the store. He swung the mop across the racks of the shelves. The power of the blows caused the shelves to fall in a row against each other, knocking down one after the next.

The customers ran out the aisles, climbing over each other as the shelves crashed to the floor. They trampled and elbowed one another, running out of the store.

Ross walked to the ice cream section of the store. He opened the freezer door and flung the ice cream to the ground. He pushed a frozen-solid, half gallon of chocolate chip ice cream with the mop, skating down the aisles in his socks.

Ross stopped.

He saw a shelf full of soup cans on each rack. Ross stood with his feet hip-width apart. He bent his knees a little and put his weight even between both feet.

He leaned forward. "Fore!"

Ross brought up the mop toward his right and then swung down to the left, hitting the ice cream towards the shelf of soup cans. The cans crashed down from the shelf and rolled around on the floor.

Police sirens were roaring outside of the store.

Ross dropped the mop. "Welp! I'm guessing those are for me!"

He looked around. There was no one left in the store. Ross kicked the items on the ground near his feet. He reached for the remote that was snugged in his back pocket.

Ross pushed the rewind button.

*****

The sun shined through the window onto Ross's face the next morning. He heard the alarm clock and rolled out of bed. His arm reached for the alarm clock in the nightstand, but it fell on his head along with the remote.

Ross picked up the remote. "I'm not going to work today. I'm going to take my magic genie for a spin!"

He put on his clothes and put the remote in his back pocket of his jeans. He headed out the front door and got into his car. Ross felt his stomach rumbling, pulling away from the driveway.

He drove to a steakhouse in town. He walked inside and took a seat on one of the diner's stools and opened a menu that was left on the table. Ross searched around for one of the servers and spotted an attractive waitress cleaning a table.

He winked at her.

The waitress came to him, taking a pencil out of her hair bun. "Hey, there! What can I get for ya?"

Ross looked down at his menu. "I would like a steak burrito with scrambled eggs."

"Sorry, but were not making any more steak," the waitress said. "Can I get you something else?"

"Wait a second!" Ross slammed the menu on the table. "So, at a steakhouse, you guys decide you're not going to make any more steak?"

"Let me double check with the head chef." The waitress hurried to the kitchen.

Not long after, the chef came out with his spatula in his hand. "Hello sir. We are out of steak. Please help yourself to anything else."

Ross caught a glimpse of the chef's face, noticing mucus and crust around his nose. The chef's hands were filthy and smelt as if he bathed in a pile of waste.

Ross turned his head away to keep from vomiting. "You're the head chef here?"

"Yes, I am."

"Just looking at you made me lose my appetite!"

"How's that?"

"You have snot hanging from your nose like a four-Year old," Ross said, "and your hands look like you've been changing tires all morning."

"Sir, if you're not going to order anything here, then leave!"

Ross pressed the pause button.

He walked to where he saw two customers who surprisingly had two juicy sirloin steaks with a large helping of garlic mashed potatoes on the side. He noticed the customers hadn't eaten them yet. They were too busy yapping and eating the complimentary bread.

Ross took both plates away from their table and went into the back of the kitchen to get two takeout containers. He grabbed a large diet soda and a piece of buttered toast from another customer's dish as we walked out the door with the food. He gobbled the buttered toast as he took the remote out of his back pocket.

Then he fast-forwarded.

*****

That afternoon, Ross took a break from his magical device. When he arrived home, he heard a strange noise. The noise sounded like scratching on a door. He followed the sound to a door that led into his garage. As soon as Ross opened the door, a tiny animal ran between his legs.

He ran in the direction of the animal, looking around the kitchen and living room. Soon, he heard whimpering coming from his bedroom. Ross walked into his bedroom and heard the animal scramble around in his closet.

He opened the closet door. A small dog with a furry coat and light-colored eyes stood on top of his worn-out sneakers.

The dog reminded Ross of a puppy that followed him home from school when he was young. He snuck the puppy inside his room when his father was at work, and his mother locked inside her makeup room.

He fed the small dog and played with it for a good while, teaching the puppy new tricks. Before long, Ross remembered he forgot to take his favorite action figure back from Glen at school. He promised the dog he would be right back and closed his bedroom door.

Ross ran down the street to Glen's home. After Glen gave him his toy, he ran back as fast as he could, smiling from ear to ear, thinking about his new pet.

When he got closer to home, he could see from afar, his father's truck pulling out the driveway. His father had come home earlier from work that evening. Ross watched him speed off in the opposite direction, and his little legs ran even faster.

He ran into the house to his room and opened the door. He didn't see the puppy. He dropped his action figure on the floor and looked all over his room, but the dog wasn't anywhere.

Ross fell to his knees with his tiny hands on his face and cried.

*****

Ross reached for the dog inside his closet, but as he came closer it backed further away. He walked into his kitchen and took out a small plastic bowl, filling it with water. He opened the fridge and took out his leftover steak from the night before and wrapped a few small pieces of it in a napkin.

He walked into his bedroom and crouched down near the closet door, placing the water bowl on the floor and opened the napkin. The dog peeked its head out of the closet and looked at the food. The dog came all the way out and nibbled at the steak in Ross's hand.

After the dog finished eating, it licked the water from the bowl. Ross slowly picked the dog up from off the ground and put it on his lap, gently stroking the dog on his head. He carried the pooch outside to his mailbox. He grabbed the few pieces of mail inside and put them in his pocket.

Ross watched as a young boy approached him with a big smile.

"Hi. Can I pet your doggy?" the boy asked.

"Uh…sure." Ross squatted down to let the child pet the dog.

The boy patted the dog on the head. "My parents said they're going to get me one."

"Do you like this one?" Ross said.

"Yes, I like the doggy!"

"Then she's all yours."

"Thank you!"

Ross placed the dog in the boy's arms, and the dog licked the child in the face. The boy smiled and walked away from Ross, carrying his new pet to his home

CHAPTER THREE

The Intruder

L**ATER THAT** evening, Ross drove to his favorite coffee shop in town. He went inside and ordered a large latte with five shots of espresso.

While drinking from his cup, he noticed a small boy sitting beside a man that looked to be his father. The man hugged the boy and let him take a few sips from his cup.

"I love you daddy." The boy stood on top of his chair and kissed his father on the forehead.

Ross stood there, watching them with tears in his eyes. Ross's father couldn't stand being in the same room with him, let alone hug him.

When he was a young schoolboy, he remembered his friends bragging about their fishing and hiking trips in the mountains with their fathers. Ross would sit there hearing their stories with his heart breaking into pieces.

Sometimes, Ross would walk to Glen's home to see if he could sneak into a movie with him but would find Glen playing a game of catch with his father in the front yard or fixing something under the car hood with him.

That wasn't Ross's reality with his father.

Through his youth, Ross thought his real name was "boy," for a long while. His father ordered him around and treated him no better than the dirt underneath his boots. His father was the most impatient man he ever knew. Everything had to be done right away. There was no waiting for his father. That world did not exist for him.

Ross dreaded thinking of the memories when his father was kept waiting too long. Often, he was smacked upside the head with the back of his father's hand for being too slow. Many times, Ross was kept from seeing friends or family, and his father would trap him inside his room for hours.

His father would punish him by taking his money or refuse to give him more to buy his lunch and Ross would starve. He begged Glen and the other kids for a share of their meals, and some days stole the lunches from the school cafeteria. If the cafeteria staff caught him, the school would call his home.

Ross's father would take off from work to drive to the school and pick him up. During their drive home, his father told him how embarrassed he was to have such a worthless, horrible son who stole food from the school. When they arrived home, Ross wasn't allowed to eat anything and sent to bed early.

As a child, Ross kept a small piggy bank in his room, saving every dime he ever got from his parents. One night, Ross remembered when his father went into his room, shouting at him. He hurled Ross's piggybank against the wall, shattering it into pieces. The backlash from the explosion struck Ross in the face. He gushed into tears from the pain.

His mother lived in her own bubble, typically, hiding in her makeup room. She never spoke a word about the chaos in their home, and for Years, Ross suffered.

The memories of his past overflowed through his mind. Ross squeezed his plastic coffee cup even tighter. He felt the warm coffee stream down his hand.

"My father has it coming to him!" Ross tossed the cup in the trash and reached for the remote from his coat pocket.

He pushed rewind.

*****

The air smelt of a musty, greasy order that bathed inside Ross's nostrils. He stood in the kitchen of his parents' home. A skillet full of cold bacon grease sat on the stove.

Ross looked down at his small hand that held the remote. He tried to put the remote in his small jean pocket, but it wouldn't fit. Ross stuffed the remote down his underwear and walked down the hallway to the bathroom.

Ross looked in the bathroom mirror.

He saw a young boy, no more than four feet tall with a full head of hair, a round face, and big eyes looking back at him. Ross could see the heartache and pain in the child's eyes, screaming for a way out of such a terrible place. Ross wanted to rescue the boy and take him back with him but knew he couldn't.

"Don't worry little guy." Ross whispered to the child staring back at him. "We'll get him!"

Ross strolled around to each room, but no one was home. He went into his father's den and looked at the calendar on the wall and the clock on the fireplace. It was an early Saturday morning, the day his mother would go to her hairdresser, and his father would take a trip to the old record store around the corner from their home.

Every once in a while, Ross caught his father in that old run-down store. Ross would hide and peek through the windows of the store to watch his father sing along to the records that played on the old jukebox, while searching for new records to buy.

Ross knew his parents would not return home until much later.

He walked into the kitchen and took the skillet from the stove burner with the leftover bacon grease and poured it into a large glass. Then, he grabbed a can of soda from the fridge.

He walked to the top of the staircase, emptying out the soda can on the top steps. He smothered the staircase's handrail with the bacon grease, wiping it down from the top of the rail all the way down to the bottom.

Afterwards, Ross went into the garage where his father stored many of his belongings on a high shelf inside cardboard boxes. Ross saw an empty crate on the floor and pushed it with his foot and hopped on top of it.

He ransacked through the boxes and found a long piece of clear wire inside one of them. Ross leaped down from the large crate, running to the storage room with the wire.

The storage was a large room surrounded by old, wobbly shelves filled with soup cans. The shelves were high to the ceiling, and the weight of the cans caused the shelves to tilt forward. Ross's father loved soup—even more than steak—and he built the storage to make sure he could never run out.

Ross wrapped the wire around the front post of a shelf and walked the wire to a shelf directly across from him. He wrapped the wire around the shelf post to connect it to both shelves. Ross checked the wire, making sure it was sturdy enough to stay in place.

Ross heard the garage door opening and a car pulling in. He peaked down the hallway.

It was his father.

*****

Ross ran into the den and opened the windows. He grabbed a pair of his father's boots that were on the floor and left out the room. Ross heard him inside the home. He put on the heavy boots and paced around a few times by the den.

"Boy?" his father said. "Is that you?"

Ross kept his mouth closed and hid out of sight.

"Say something, you little runt!" His father walked into the den and laid his new records on top of the television.

Ross saw his father catch sight of the window, wide open.

His father put his head outside the window. He looked around. Then locked the window shut and searched around the den. His father grabbed the neck of a wine bottle from off the floor. He flipped the bottle upside down to use as a weapon, holding it near his head.

Ross stomped the boots in the kitchen and crammed himself into one of the large kitchen cabinets. He peeked out the cabinet door, watching his father tiptoe out of the den with the wine bottle clutched in his hand, opening the door that led into the hallway.

His father then walked into the kitchen—barely inches away from the cabinet that Ross hid in—looking inside the broom closet. Soon, his father left the kitchen towards the hallway.

Ross slowly opened the cabinet door wider, watching his father move further down the hall. Ross climbed out of the cabinet, running as fast as he could to the staircase and thumped his feet on the steps, and slid into the coat closet.

Ross's father ran in the direction of the staircase, waving the bottle of wine in his hand. He ran up the stairs and slipped on the soda. He reached for the handrail, but the bacon greased caused it to slip from his hand and he tumbled down to the end of the staircase.

Ross heard the racket and cracked the closet door open. His father lay flat on his back with the shattered pieces of the wine bottle, and the spilled wine all over the staircase. Ross put his hand over his mouth and giggled.

After a few minutes, he watched his father stand up, stumbling over himself on the stairs, and limp down the hallway.

Ross ran out the closet into the storage room and stomped his feet on the ground.

"Whoever you are!" his father shouted." I'm coming to get you!"

Ross hid behind the door.

His father hobbled into the storage room and his leg pushed against the wire.

The top of the shelves fell forward, crashing into each other. Soup cans and boxes shot from the shelves right on top of him. His father cried out, falling to the ground.

Ross moved from behind the storage door. He watched his father squirming around on the floor with his eyes closed.

Suddenly, Ross heard the front door open and close. He heard footsteps walking around near the front of the house.

A woman screamed.

The footsteps traveled faster down the hallway into the storage.

"Chester!" Ross's mother ran to him. "What happened here?"

"Alice…" Chester said.

"Yes, Chester?"

"…That burglar…"

"What burglar? There was a burglar?"

"That burglar… sure got me good!" his father passed out.

"Ross!" His mother screamed. "Get an ambulance!"

"He'll be alright!" Ross giggled.

Ross took off his father's shoes and puffed his chest out, strutting in his socks into the bathroom. He climbed to the top of the sink, staring at the little boy in the mirror. A big grin beamed from the boy's face. The child took the remote from out his underwear.

He pressed fast forward.

*****

That night, Ross heard someone banging on his door. He looked out of the window and opened the door.

"Hey, Glen. What's going on?"

"Why haven't you returned my calls?"

"What calls?"

"Very funny!" Glen pushed open the door.

"I've been busy." Ross closed the door behind him.

"Have you been using the remote without me?"

"And if I have?" Ross said.

"We agreed that we were going to use it together."

"I had other plans." Ross pounced on the sofa.

Glen stared at Ross.

"By the way, I destroyed a supermarket," Ross said.

"And you're not behind bars?"

"I pressed the rewind button just in time."

"Ross, you can't—"

"Oh, and I went and got my dad back too, and a bunch of other stuff."

"You're going to wear that thing out," Glen said.

"I doubt that! This remote was sent by the universe."

"Where is the remote?"

'It's resting comfortably in my leather bag."

"Screwing with that thing could affect the past and future somehow."

"Who cares!" Ross crossed his feet on the coffee table.

"I was around on your first trip." Glen paced back and forth. "So, why haven't I've been tagging along?"

"I don't know. Maybe, you were too far away."

"We should try to figure out how close I need to be."

"Nope!" Ross said.

"Why not?"

"If you're there, cool. If you're not, even better."

"You said you wanted to fast forward to the good stuff."

"Sure did."

"But it seems like you're only rewinding from all the bad stuff you're getting yourself into!"

"That's right." Ross smiled. "I can do whatever I want."

"Why won't you use that thing to see how life evolves hundreds of Years from now?"

"We've already went to the future once," Ross said. "I'm not interested in doing it again."

"Then how about going back in time to speak with Abraham Lincoln? Or checking out the Stone Age?"

"Yea, I think I'll pass."

"Why?"

"Because my ideas are way better than yours."

"We have something incredible and you're using it to self-destruct in grocery stores."

"Kaboooom!" Ross laughed.

"I cannot believe this!" Glen walked away.

"Now, where do you think you're going?"

Glen turned around. "I need to use your bathroom if that's okay with you?"

"Go right ahead," Ross said. "You know where it is."

*****

Ross knew Glen was upset with him. Then again, this wasn't the first time he and Glen got into an argument, and it wouldn't be the last.

Ross met Glen before he knew how to tie his own shoes. As kids, he fought off bullies with Glen and copied his homework in class. Ross pranked his teachers with him, burping during class or placing a Whoopi cushion on the seat of their chairs.

Ross didn't have any siblings of his own, and Glen was the only boy with four older sisters. So, one day at school, Ross took a blood oath with Glen, promising each other to be best friends and brothers, forever.

From time to time, Ross invited Glen over to his home after school. Ross's father would always yell at him and call him names. Glen told Ross he wanted to help him get away from his father and planned an escape route for him.

One day, Glen brought him a drawing of a map, unfolding it on top of his bed. While Glen explained his escape plan, Ross could hear someone by his door, snooping around. His father burst into his room and snatched the drawing off his bed. He told Glen to get out of his house and ripped the map into shreds.

Ross grew older, becoming more like his father. As a result, he and Glen would argue more often, and he wouldn't talk to Glen for long periods at a time. Though, somehow, Ross would always come back as friends with him again.

Ross believed Glen still cherished the memories of them climbing trees, chasing squirrels, and riding their bikes together the same as Ross did. Or maybe, Glen wanted to honor his blood oath he made to him long ago. Whatever it was, Ross knew Glen loved him like a brother.

Ross turned on his television and took a sip from his soda can but couldn't help but think about the remote. Glen decided to let it rest in his leather bag until he got to work in the morning.

*****

Meanwhile, inside his bathroom, his best friend Glen, had other plans.

Glen turned on the sink, splashing water on his face, and dried it with a hand towel. He walked out the bathroom, noticing Ross's leather bag sitting on top of the dresser.

Ross doesn't need something like that.

Glen took the leather bag off the dresser and dug inside for the remote. He took it out and put it inside his pants pocket. Then he put the leather bag back on the dresser.

"Did you fall in the toilet?" Ross opened the bedroom door. "Why didn't you use the guestroom bathroom?"

"Because I'm not a guest." Glen made a wide circle around Ross, heading for the door. "I have to get going. Charlotte's waiting for me at the house."

Glen hurried home. He did not see Charlotte's car parked in the driveway. He walked inside to the bedroom and closed the door. He took the remote out of his pocket and sat on top of the bed.

His mind wandered.

Glen's eyes roamed over the history books on his shelf, thinking of the Kings and Queens that lived before him, and the great dinosaurs that once walked the earth. He fantasized about the evolving of mankind and life beyond the galaxies.

The remote trembled in his hand. He stood up from the bed and his thoughts suffocated him.

There's so much to see. I don't know where to begin...

CHAPTER FOUR

Fight Night

THE NEXT morning, Ross fell out of bed and glanced up at the clock on his dresser. He was late for work, again. He went into his closet to take out his work clothes.

Then he stopped.

Ross closed the closet door. He walked to his dresser and took out his underwear and favorite pajamas, strolling into the bathroom for a long shower.

When he was finished, he put on his pajamas and his flip-flops that were near the bedroom door and reached for his leather bag on top of the dresser. Then he went out to his car.

When Ross arrived at work, he could hear the snickering of his coworkers from afar, watching him from their cubicles. He walked inside with his sandals flapping against his feet, approaching his coworkers' desks. He started to walk past them but remembered the magic remote inside his leather bag.

Today, he wasn't going to ignore them.

Ross walked toward his giggling coworkers, Eddy and Pearl—the leaders of the gossip box—and stopped right in front of them.

Ross put on the biggest, fakest smile he could muster. "Hey, guys!"

"Hey, Ross!" Eddy burst into laughter. "I just love the outfit."

"You're actually talking to us?" Pearl said.

"Well, why wouldn't I?" Ross said. "I heard you laughing hyenas all the way down the hall!"

"Excuse me?" Pearl said.

"Oh, you're excused," Ross said. "Did you let one fly again?"

Pearl covered her mouth with her hand.

Ross leaned over her cubicle. "You have a terrible habit of doing that!"

Ross walked away, leaving his coworkers' mouths wide-open. He didn't hear anyone laughing anymore, flapping his flip-flops down the hallway.

Jonas came out of his office, blocking the walkway to tie his shoes.

"I don't know what's worse," Ross said. "Waiting for you or standing in line at the DMV!"

"Sorry!" Jonas moved out of Ross's way.

Ross went into his office and put his leather bag on his desk. Then he walked to the breakroom near his office. Myra and Susan were in front of the watercooler, gossiping and cackling. Ross stood next to them, pouring a cup of coffee.

"The schools are out today," Susan said. "That's why traffic was pretty good this morning."

"Really?" Myra said. "My husband works for a school. He was getting dressed for work today."

"That's strange," Susan said. "There is no school today. Maybe, he was—"

"Don't worry, Myra," Ross said. "I'm sure he's at home, you know, painting your house."

The two women watched Ross laugh all the way to his office.

Ross walked into his office and put the cup down on his desk. He heard someone breathing behind him and turned around.

"Morning," Bennet said. "Nice pajamas!"

Ross looked at him. "Are you allergic to knocking?"

"Sorry, but I wanted to show you something."

"What is it?"

"Can't you see?"

"See, what?"

"The changes!"

"What changes?"

"I'm slimmer. Can't you tell?"

Ross chuckled. "I've been hearing about this for a while now."

"I know, but—"

"I have yet to see any results."

"So, what do you think I should do?"

"Just throw in the towel!" Ross laughed. "Just kidding!"

Then he walked out of his office with his sandals slapping against his feet.

*****

It was almost noon. The meeting with Mr. Mallard would soon begin. He was the biggest client that the company serviced, and the most annoying. There wasn't a day that Mr. Mallard didn't complain when he came to the office.

Before he came inside, he would send his assistants to test the room temperature with thermometers. If it was not exactly sixty-two degrees, he would refuse to come inside. To satisfy Mr. Mallard's request, the company set a policy in place; It stated employees were not allowed to touch the thermostat or bring heaters into the office.

He demanded to have his massage therapist present for foot rubs, and back rubs between meetings more than an hour long. He requested that hot tea be served from a steaming kettle with two slices of fresh lemon and poured to him in the finest of glassware.

Even so, the company made great effort to assure him that the office was beyond cleanliness. Mr. Mallard would still bring his own team of custodians to disinfect everything.

Ross hated Mr. Mallard. He was invited to the afternoon meeting with him, but Ross wasn't interested in the least bit. He peeped through the windows of the conference room where Mr. Mallard's assistants and massage therapist sat, but Ross did not see him.

Good. Maybe, the rascal had to leave.

Ross walked down the hall, but Mr. Mallard caught him as he came out of the bathroom.

When Ross saw Mr. Mallard, his face scrunched up, and he covered his mouth to keep from vomiting all over his expensive suit.

"Ross," Mr. Mallard said. "Aren't you joining us in the meeting?"

Ross looked at him.

Mr. Mallard glanced at Ross's pajamas and flip-flops. "Did the office have a sleepover last night?"

Ross just stared at him.

"Didn't you hear me ask you a question?"

Ross rolled his eyes and sighed. "Do you need something, Mr. Mallard?"

"Actually, I do."

"How can I help you?"

"My pen dropped in the toilet," Mr. Mallard said. "Can you go fetch it for me?"

"No problem," Ross said. "Would you like me to roll out the red carpet for you too?"

"I beg your pardon?"

"I noticed your team of servants are not surrounding you."

"My team of servants?"

"I'm surprised you're even walking. Aren't you usually carried around everywhere?"

"You can't speak to me like this!" Mr. Mallard got up in Ross's face. "Didn't you get the memo about who I am?"

Ross looked dead into his eyes. "Yes, I did, and you definitely live up to your name."

"And what might that be?"

"A quacking duck!"

Ross flapped his sandals away from Mr. Mallard and walked into his office. He sat down in his chair, reaching for his leather bag on his desk.

"Ross!" Tank shouted. "In my office, now!"

"You got it!" Ross put his leather bag down and followed behind Tank.

Tank walked into his office. "Close the door behind you."

Ross closed the door and took a seat in front of Tank's desk.

Tank was one of the highest executives in the company, and he made sure that anyone who stepped into his spacious office knew it. The curtains that hung on the windows were open, giving his office a soft, warm glow. Tank's portraits of classical art hung on the walls near his college degrees and countless awards.

"What's the problem, Tank?" Ross crossed his feet on top of Tank's desk.

Tank looked at Ross's feet on his desk. He grabbed his cup on the desk, sipped from it, and placed it back down. He took two long, deep breaths.

“Had fun playing hooky?” Tank said. “I see you finally showed up for work."

“It was a nice little vacation,” Ross said.

“You've never been an employee that's given one hundred percent.”

“You'll get a hundred percent from me when my salary starts to show it.” Ross put his hands behind his head and leaned back in the chair.

Tank walked to the front of his desk and crossed his arms. “I've gotten quite a few complaints filed on you today.”

"Oh? What else is new?"

"One from our biggest client."

"I guess speaking your mind is—"

"Mr. Mallard said he may cancel our contract."

"And where is he going to go?" Ross said. "We're the only firm that's silly enough to put up with him."

Tank looked down at Ross's sandals. "Are you aware of our company dress code?"

"I'm very aware." Ross smiled, wiggling his toes.

"Judging from your outfit and the trouble you've caused today, I'm going to assume you're—"

"I'm perfectly fine."

"Yeah, right!" Tank slapped Ross's feet from off his desk.

Ross gave Tank a big smile, showing him all his teeth.

"You have got to be the worst employee I've ever had," Tank said.

"Well, what a surprise!"

"You know what needs to happen to useless employees like you?"

"What needs to happen? Tell me, Tanky."

"We need to take a big, long rope and—"

Ross grabbed Tank's coffee mug and accidentally sloshed the remaining coffee toward him.

"What the!" Tank said as a few drops splashed across his face. He stumbled backward and quickly wiped his eyes.

"Hey, sorry about that!" Ross smirked. "Those darn reflexes!"

"You're fired!" Tank, barely able to see, picked up his phone receiver. "We need security up here, now!"

Ross jumped up, dancing out of Tank's office. He danced all the way down the hall, shaking his fanny while his sandals popped against his heels. Everyone watched him. Some clapped at his dance moves.

Ross danced all the way to his office as they all followed behind him. He grabbed his leather bag from off his desk, left his office, and climbed up a desk in an empty cubicle, so he could see out over the whole office.

The office gathered around him as he showcased the leather bag as security charged through the crowd.

"Come down off the table, Ross," a security officer said.

"You people are the worst!" Ross pointed his finger at them. "Many of you dedicated your lives to make me miserable here!"

"We're not asking again," the guard said.

"You can't do anything to me! I have—"

Ross opened the bag and put his hand inside.

The remote was gone.

Before he could say a word, his body was thrown to the ground. The guards lifted him by his clothes and hauled him out of the office. Ross kicked and screamed as security threw him outside, landing him on his backside.

His leather bag soared in the air, thumping against his head. Ross lay there, holding a hand against the swelling lump behind his ear where the bag had clipped it.

*****

That afternoon, Ross searched through his home, yanking out every drawer in the kitchen. He looked in the oven, the pantries, and inside the dishwasher. He ripped the cushions from the chairs and the sofa. He checked inside the hallway closet, and then to his bedroom. He searched under the bed, inside his dirty clothes hamper and the shelves in his closet.

Ross walked to the front porch and then to the backyard looking around for the remote. He walked back into the house and emptied out the trash cans on the floor, looking through the garbage.

"Where is it?!" Ross shouted. "This doesn't make any sense!"

Ross sat down on his sofa with his hands on his face. Then, he sank to the ground with his arms stretched out wide and his face pressed against the cold, hard floor. "I cannot believe this is happening to me."

There came a knock on his front door.

"It's open!" Ross yelled.

Glen opened the door and let himself inside.

"What's the matter?" Glen laughed. "Did one of your girlfriends find out about the other one?"

"I can't find it anywhere."

"Find what?" Glen asked. "Your sanity?"

"No. The remote."

Glen helped Ross up from the floor and placed him on the sofa.

"I have looked everywhere for it, but it's gone," Ross said. "I think it vanished away with its magical powers."

"I took the remote," Glen said.

"What did you say?"

"You weren't doing sensible things with it."

"It wasn't yours to take!"

"You were busy trashing supermarkets. I had a better use for it."

Ross jumped off the couch with his fist rolled up tight. "I got fired today and couldn't rewind!"

"You got fired?" Glen chuckled. "Well, it's about time!"

"Where is it, Glen?"

"You, of all people, don't need to have something like that."

"Don't tell me what I need!"

Glen noticed Ross tightening his other fist. "How about you come over to my house tonight? I'll grab the remote when we get there."

Ross loosened his fists. "Charlotte is going to be okay with this?"

"I'll talk to her," Glen said. "She'll be fine."

*****

The two drove over to Glen's home. Glen took his car keys from the ignition and got out of the car with Ross. From a distance, they could see the front door slightly open. When they came closer, they noticed a pair of eyeballs peeking from the doorway.

When Ross approached the door, it swung open and almost hit him dead in the face.

"WOAH!" Ross blocked his face with his hands, stumbling backwards.

Charlotte rushed toward Glen. "What is this maniac doing here?"

"Maniac?" Ross yelled. "Whose clobbering folks with front doors?"

"Charlotte," Glen said, "I invited him over to—"

Charlotte slid past Glen towards Ross. "Myra told me what you said to her earlier."

"Oh, right!" Ross sighed. "I forgot you two know each other."

"She's my best friend!" Charlotte said. "The manager was right for throwing you right on your—"

"Charlotte, cut it out!" Glen said. "Ross had a long day and so have I."

"Fine! I'll make us something to eat." Charlotte went inside.

Ross rubbed his forehead. "Your wife needs a—"

"Don't start with her," Glen said. "I don't need any more fireworks tonight."

Ross and Glen walked inside.

Glen placed his keys on the television stand. "Let's have a Blackjack while we wait for Charlotte."

"I just want the remote, so I can get out of here." Ross said.

"Don't be silly!" Glen said.

"When are you giving me the remote?"

"After we eat. I'll grab it for you." Glen left to the patio room.

Ross stood waiting for Glen and looked at Charlotte.

"Hey, Charlotte. Thanks for cooking up some grub."

Charlotte squinted her eyes at him. "Uh, huh."

Glen brought in a foldup card table and two chairs from the patio room, giving the two chairs to Ross. Glen unfolded the table in the living room and wiped the dust off with a paper towel. They sat down and played two games, and Glen cut the deck for the third game.

"I'm sick of playing." Ross scooted his chair away from the table. "You beat me twice already."

"You want to do something else?"

"I want the remote back!"

"But we have one last game," Glen said. "Besides, I think you should let me hang on to it."

"What?!" Ross shouted.

Charlotte looked over at them with her arms crossed. "What's going on over there?"

"Nothing, dear." Glen turned to face her. "I'm beating the socks off Ross on the scoreboard."

"You said you would give it back!" Ross said.

"Keep it down, will ya?" Glen whispered.

"No, I'm not! You said—"

"Here you guys, go!" Charlotte said.

She brought two big, round bowls to their table, and gave them both each a spoon wrapped in a napkin.

Ross stared inside his bowl. "Is this some kind of white chili?"

"No," Charlotte said. "It's scallop potatoes."

Ross took the spoon out of the napkin and dipped it into the bowl. "Is mine poisoned by chance?"

Charlotte took a deep breath and bit her bottom lip.

"Honey, he's kidding," Glen said.

Ross stirred the potatoes. He scooped up two small chunks into his mouth.

He spat them back out.

"Good grief, Charlotte!" Ross said. "Ever heard of takeout?"

"Ross!" Glen yelled.

"I've been waiting to tell her that for Years," Ross said.

Charlotte burst into tears and ran into the bedroom, slamming the door.

"She didn't deserve that!" Glen shouted.

Ross scrubbed his tongue with the napkin. "I hope I got it all out of my mouth."

"Get out of my house!" Glen jumped out of his chair, flipping over the table.

Ross leaped out of the way just in time. "This wouldn't have happened in the first place, if you would've kept your sticky fingers out of my leather bag!"

"You're losing it, bro!" Glen yelled. "You're acting as if you're the God of Time."

"I am. We both are!"

"That's it. You're not getting the remote back."

"You're gonna go get it, Glen!"

"I'm not getting you anything."

Ross charged at Glen, knocking him down to the floor. The two men wrestled each other on the ground. Ross quickly put one arm over Glen's neck. He reached his other arm in from under Glen's arm, hooking his hands together in a tight grip over his chest.

Ross and Glen pushed each other back and forth, crashing into the television stand, and it fell on top of them. The collision caused the walls to tremble, and the remote dropped down from under a large painting that was hanging above them.

Charlotte ran out of the bedroom. "Get off my husband!"

She grabbed the remote from off the floor, smacking Ross over the head with it.

"Stop hitting me!" Ross looked up at Charlotte.

"The remote!"

Ross let go of Glen, chasing after Charlotte. She ran away to the bedroom and threw the remote to the ground. Ross picked the remote from off the floor, but Glen snatched it from behind him, running out of the house.

Glen got to his car and checked his pockets for his keys.

"Are you looking for these?" Ross shook the keys.

Glen ran as fast as he could down the street into an empty alley. It was dark, and the streetlights hadn't yet come on.

The alley was a dead end.

Suddenly, Ross grabbed Glen's legs from behind, slamming Glen on his stomach.

"Get off me!" Glen yelled.

Ross jerked at the remote in Glen's hand. "Give it back!"

"No!"

The two rolled on the ground, tugging and pulling on the remote.

The red light on top of the remote blinked rapidly. Suddenly, their vision darkened, and the room whirled around at a dramatic speed.

Ross blacked out.

CHAPTER FIVE

Endless Silence

ROSS AWOKE onto a dirt road. The rays of the scorching sun rested on his skin.

Glen kicked Ross's leg from on top of him. "Get away from me!"

Ross kicked him back. "You shouldn't have stolen from me."

"You're a menace!" Glen yelled.

Ross looked around, picking himself up from the ground. He noticed poorly built huts surrounding a city that were made from mud and clay. The roofs of the huts were bounded with straws. From a distance, he could see farmers, harvesting their crops with scarves wrapped around their heads. Some of the people nearby were riding on top of camels.

"Where are we?" Ross asked.

“I don’t know,” Glen said. “Isn’t this stuff from your imagination?”

“Nope,” Ross said.

“Are you sure this isn’t a random place inside your head?”

“This place isn’t from my past or imagination.”

“Well, it’s not from mine either!” Glen walked away.

Ross followed behind him.

“You go that way, and I’ll got this way!” Glen yelled.

“We have to stick together,” Ross said.

"Are you kidding me?" Glen said. "I don't want to be anywhere near you!"

Ross picked up the remote from the ground. "We broke it. The buttons are stuck."

Glen stopped and turned around. "So, this is some weird glitch of that thing?"

"We're in the remote's imagination." Ross placed the remote in his pocket.

"This is just great!" Glen paced with his hands behind his head.

They decided to wander through the city. Journeying further, the people stared and laughed at them.

"What's so funny?" Ross said.

"Something is making them laugh at us," Glen said.

"What do you think it is?"

Glen put his hands on his hips and stared toward the ground.

"What's going on in that noggin of yours?" Ross said.

"It's our clothes!"

"What about them?"

"We don't fit in."

Ross looked down at his pants. "You're probably right."

They traveled further and came upon a fish market up the road. There was a trader selling clothing and wine nearby. Ross and Glen walked toward the seller.

The man was tiny and very thin. His hair was pulled back into a ponytail, and he wore a scarf that hung from his head. The man's clothes were dirty and he wore no shoes. It looked like he hadn't slept in days.

Ross looked at his clothing on the display. "We need clothes."

The man looked at him and scratched his head.

Ross slapped his hands together. "Hello!"

The man shook his head and murmured something under his breath.

"He doesn't understand us," Glen said.

Ross flung his arms in the air. "Oh great! Do you have any idea what language he's speaking?"

"Not a clue," Glen said.

"We need these!" Ross looked at the seller, pointing at the clothes.

The small man watched Ross point his finger at the garments. Then he picked up the clothing and whispered something.

"I don't know what he's saying," Ross said.

The seller rubbed his fingers together.

"I think I got it now," Glen said.

"What?"

"He wants some moolah!"

"Of course, he does," Ross said. "Do you have any cash on you?"

Out of the blue, three other men approached the seller and looked at the clothing on the display. They took from their pockets what looked like goods that were grown from their farms.

Ross watched the men bargain with the seller.

"Our money is not what they use here," Glen said.

"So, what now?"

"I'm just as stumped as you are."

Within minutes, a peaceful negotiation with the seller for his goods quickly launched into a roaring argument. One of the traders seized the seller by the throat and lifted him off the ground, shaking him high in the air. The other two men crowded around them, pulling out their daggers.

Ross, noticing the men were distracted, stole the garments and ran away. Glen, right behind him, followed him through the dirt road. They came to a stop and hid behind a large mud-brick wall. Ross looked around to see if the men had followed them.

"Nice move!" Glen said.

"Quick. Put these on." Ross threw some of the clothing at Glen.

They put on the clothes and wrapped the scarves around their heads, and Ross slid the remote in his scarf.

*****

Traveling further through the dirt streets, Ross grew thirsty and tired as the sun beamed down on his thick clothing. Soon, he and Glen came upon a crowd being served wine and bread. They hurried toward the crowd to receive a share of the food.

Sitting in the middle of the crowd were four men with colorful garments tied around their heads. Their legs were crossed on top of an old, tattered blanket. All of them wore long sleeve shirts with a vest, pants, and bright beaded necklaces. In front of them were wicker baskets, which were covered with lids made from bamboo trees.

The crowd grew quiet as one of the men approached each basket and chanted. He blew his breath on top of the lids and sat down on the blanket, signaling to have the lids removed from the baskets.

The lids were quickly taken off.

The four men took out their flute-like instruments, playing a beautifully decorative tune, soaking the crowd's ears with enchantment, causing them to shiver with goosebumps. The crowd sang and danced, putting feathers and money on the musicians' blankets.

The vipers rose from the baskets, swaying to the exotic instruments. The music hypnotized the snakes, leading them into a dazed trance.

Suddenly, a mysterious woman appeared within the crowd. She wore gold earrings and a sheer lavender woven top with long sleeves. Her high slit lavender skirt was trimmed with satin lace, and a lavender sash was tied tightly around her waist. The woman's hair flowed down her back, and a lavender veil hung from her face.

Her eyes spotted Ross.

Ross caught the woman staring at him. He watched her take something out of her bustier. It looked like a root from a plant. Looking directly at him, she held it in the air and wiggled it. At that moment, the woman put the root in her mouth and ate it.

Ross vomited to the ground.

Glen rushed to him. "Are you alright?"

Ross wiped his mouth with his hand. "I think so."

The woman remained calm, approaching one of the wicker baskets. Ross watched her take one of the vipers away from one of them. She gently grasped it firmly in her hands. Ross saw the crowd marvel at the woman because the snake did not bite her.

The woman moved her hips to the beat of the music, gently turning and spinning slowly with the snake, holding it carefully above her head. The crowd clapped and cheered while the snake slithered around, harmonizing itself with her.

Ross watched the woman dance with the viper, allowing the serpent to explore her body. Ross felt a surge of blood rush into his brain. Sensations of fear, happiness, sadness, anger, and love rippled through him. He couldn't feel his body moving, and his eyes were fixed on the woman.

Ross's body sank to the ground.

"Ross!" Glen yelled. "What's wrong?"

"Its her."

"Who?"

"The Siren of Pisces."

Ross pointed at the mysterious woman dancing with the viper. "She wants to synchronize with me."

Glen looked back towards her. "Let her synchronize with somebody else!"

"No, wait. She—"

Glen lifted Ross from the ground. "We have to figure out how to get out of here!"

The woman stopped dancing and carefully placed the viper back into the basket.

Ross could hear someone behind them and looked back. It was the snake woman.

Ross's eyes met with hers, feeling his body recover. The woman walked closer but stopped.

She reached out her hand to Ross.

Tears poured down Ross's face. "I don't have any money, my love."

"My love?" Glen said.

Ross took the remote out of his scarf. "But I have something else for you."

"What are you doing?!" Glen yelled.

The woman took the remote from him and ran.

Ross chased after her.

"Get back here, Ross!" Glen ran after him.

"No!"

"You have no idea where she's taking you!"

"It doesn't matter," Ross said. "She wants me!"

*****

He chased the woman until she disappeared in the dark shadows of the city. Ross looked around for her. "Where did she go?"

Glen stopped behind him, wheezing out of breath. "You have finally lost all your marbles!"

"I couldn't let her go," Ross said. "I'm in love with her."

"You, in love?" Glen's mouth flew open. "You have got to be under a magical spell."

"We have to find her," Ross said.

Glen grabbed Ross and shook him. "Wake up, man!"

He pushed Glen away from him, running through the curving, maze-like streets of the city. Ross heard an echo of laughter surrounding him and stopped. He looked down and saw a trail of red spots that looked like blood. Ross went to follow the trail of blood, but three men grabbed him from behind.

"Let me go!" Ross screamed.

Ross looked at the two men who held him and recognized them immediately. They were the men from the fish market who had argued with the seller.

Another two men came from a dark corner of the street. They approached them with Glen gagged and bound in their hands.

"Glen, are you okay?" Ross asked.

Glen shook his head.

One of the men who held Ross put a dagger to his throat.

A woman appeared from the darkest corner of the city, wearing a purple veil around her face. It was the same woman who had danced with the viper.

The woman walked slowly down the dirt road. She held her head upright, moving her arms ever so slightly by her side. She gazed at them, smiling with her eyes, and the trail of blood on the dirt street absorbed under her feet.

Ross watched her approach the men who held Glen. The woman said something to the men in their language, taking the remote from the sash around her waist.

The men shoved Ross and Glen to the floor, fascinated by the strange object in the woman's hand. They took gifts from their pockets and placed them at her feet. The woman laughed with blood streaming from under her veil, swaying the remote around in her hand.

Ross no longer felt spellbound by the woman. The shackles of his love for her were gone. Ross jumped off the ground, running towards the woman and leaped at her, snatching the remote from her hand. He dived down, tumbling along the ground. He slammed the remote down with every ounce of his strength.

The woman commanded the men to take out their weapons. The men readied their daggers and took him by the throat. Ross took one last glance at the remote in his hand.

The red light came on.

*****

The sounds of howling wolves awoke Ross. His face was pressed against a blanket of rotting leaves and broken twigs. The bright moon peered through the dusky, blue sky over his face, breathing the cold air through his nostrils.

Ross stood up from the ground and stumbled around. He watched Glen, still gagged and bound, open his eyes. Ross went to him and took off the ropes around his mouth and hands.

"Where are we now?" Glen said.

Ross held the remote in his hand. "It looks like were someplace in the middle of the woods."

"This is just great!" Glen sighed.

Ross looked at the remote. "The buttons are still stuck."

"Let's walk around and try to figure out this madness!" Glen said.

Ross noticed the sounds from the wolves were calm, and silence fell upon them. The earth became gloomier and his eyes slowly adjusted to the darkness. Ross and Glen picked up their pace with the crunching of stiff leaves under their feet.

Minutes later, it was undeniably dark, and the air was colder, and the road melted into blackness. The wind carried the fragrance of damp dirt and old fallen leaves.

*****

Wandering further down the road, it seemed to be some life in the woods. Multitudes of glowing eyes beamed through the darkness. Ross's heart pounded, believing the eyes were those of wolves. The glowing eyes in the night followed them through the woods.

"These wolves are after us," Ross said. "We're surrounded!"

"Keep your voice down." Glen whispered. "Try the remote again."

Ross punched the remote. "It's still not working!"

Ross saw something moving in the distance, just visible through the trees ahead of them. He stopped and picked up a large stick as he tried to make out the shadowy image.

It came closer.

The shadowy figure approached them. It seemed like a typical human walking with two legs. The legs grew into four, eight, and somehow back at two, bending sideways. When the legs grew to eight, they looked like knotted, crawling fingers. The long, lop-sided limbs of the being allowed it to dart suddenly in any direction.

Ross threw down his stick and ran in the opposite direction with Glen. The eyes that followed them, which once gleamed the golden rays, were now the color of red. The eyes blinked throughout the darkness of the woods, growing larger.

Ross could feel his flesh tingling.

*****

They ran far down the road, and there was a cabin not too far ahead. They ran up the crumbling porch of the cabin through the entrance of the door.

The cabin was empty, and its logs were old and cracked with age. There was a boarded window on each of the walls. The floor was decked with broken pieces of wood, which had fallen from the ceiling.

Cobwebs were spread along the ceiling and a shaft of light passed through the decaying rooftop. On the other side of the room, rusty nails poked out of the handles of the drooping cabinets. It looked like, at one time, someone could have lived there.

Perhaps, they still did.

The two friends hid there for what seemed like eternity. There was nothing but silence, and the breeze of the wind blowing against the walls of the cabin.

Ross stood there, soaking with fear. Things were getting worse at every passing moment. From the strange woman that wore the purple veil to the shadowy image of a two-legged being that could transform into an eight-legged creature.

What did this all mean? Ross believed everything happened for a reason. The remote the strange woman left on his porch was no mistake.

He thought about all the people he hurt in his life. All the rotten things he said and done because of his rage. He was turning into the very thing he feared the most.

His father.

Glen waved his hand in Ross's face. "Is somebody in there?"

"Yeah. I hope so," Ross said.

"You were just standing there, staring into space," Glen said.

"I screwed all this up!" Ross slid down to the floor.

"I'm glad you finally get it." Glen grabbed Ross's hand, helping him off the floor.

"You think we're ok?" Ross asked.

"Maybe," Glen said. "Whatever that was would've got us by now."

"I'll look outside to see what's going on." Ross walked to the door.

"Just take a peek," Glen said. "Don't put your whole face out there."

"I know what to do!" Ross turned the handle of the door.

The handle would not turn.

Ross pulled the handle back. It didn't budge.

"It's stuck!" Ross yelled.

"Use more pressure to open it," Glen said.

Ross shoved the door with the force of his shoulder.

Still, it did not open.

Glen walked over to Ross and turned the handle of the door. When he realized it was stuck, he slammed his body against the door.

"I'll keep trying the door," Glen said. "Go and try the windows."

Ross walked to the window and pushed up against it. "Same thing!"

"Let's use our weight to open the door," Glen said.

Ross walked to the door. "Let's charge it. Maybe, that will work!"

"Okay. On three," Glen said. "One...two... three!"

They charged the door, shoving against it. The door shoved them back, tossing them to the other side of the cabin. They soared headfirst into the cabinets that broke their fall.

For a few moments, Ross felt his body zapped of energy. He grabbed his head with both hands. "What just happened?"

Glen's body was shaking. "Something is blocking that door!"

"Oh, no. Please don't say that," Ross said.

"There's no way that door could have handled that impact," Glen said.

"Are you sure it's not just stuck?"

"Stuck?" Glen rubbed the side of his head. "We just bolted across the room!"

"I know. It was insane!"

"Whatever that is has been out there—waiting."

"Waiting for what?" Ross said. "It won't let us leave!"

"Then, maybe, it's coming in."

*****

Ross and Glen picked themselves up from the ground. The air in the room started to grow muggy and warm. The cabin had no electric wiring, nor did it have a furnace built inside of it. The heat in the room increased and sweat poured down their faces.

"My shirt is soaked," Ross said.

"Mine is too." Glen walked around the cabin.

"Is it a fire?"

"It can't be." Glen sniffed the air. "I don't smell anything burning."

Ross looked up at the ceiling, and it was nearly at the top of his head.

"Glen!" Ross shouted. "Look at the ceiling!"

Glen looked upwards with his nose almost touching the tip of the roof. "How in the world did—"

"The room is shrinking!" Ross ducked his head from the ceiling.

Ross looked to the left of him and then to the right. The sides of the cabin walls were closer.

"The heat… I can't take it!" Glen fell to his knees and ripped off his shirt.

"Glen, are you okay?" Ross hit his head on the ceiling and fell to his knees.

The walls were moving closer toward them. They both crawled to their knees over to one side of the room. Ross watched Glen lay on the floor, breathing slowly.

The ceiling moved further down.

Ross removed his shirt. "Glen, I'm going to try the remote!"

He took the remote from his back pocket, slamming it against the wall beside him. The ceiling was lowering to his head, and the walls moved in closer. Ross slammed the remote against the floor, gagging from his vomit. His thoughts circled from the time he first discovered the remote.

I wish I could go back. I would've never opened that box!

Suddenly, everything went black.

*****

Ross opened his eyes. He was standing inside a decayed version of his own house. The city outside was silent. Cars were abandoned in the streets. Buildings were collapsing. The sky was dim and gray.

He walked past the mirror hanging on the living room wall and caught a glimpse of himself. An old man stared back at him, his face carved with deep wrinkles and streaks of gray running through his hair. His dead, soulless eyes looked back at him.

Ross stumbled backward in shock and crashed to the floor. Something dug into his back. He reached beneath him and pulled it out.

It was the remote.

It had been broken clean in half, its buttons scattered and missing.

Ross slowly climbed to his feet and searched the old house, calling out for Glen. He searched every room, then wandered into the backyard, but there was no sign of him.

Hoping someone had survived, Ross made his way to Harvey's house next door.

But the house was gone.

All that remained was a pile of weathered lumber and splintered boards, as if the home had been abandoned decades ago.

"Hello!" Ross shouted. "Is anybody there?"

His voice echoed through the empty neighborhood before fading into silence. But no one answered. He was completely alone, an old man with no one left in the world to confide in.

Ross stood in the middle of the empty street. There was no traffic. No shouting. No buzzing street lights.

No people anywhere.

The city stretched for miles beneath a dead gray sky. Cars sat abandoned in intersections with their doors hanging open. Store windows were shattered and covered in dust. Buildings stood hollow and silent like giant tombs.

Not even the wind moved.

Ross walked slowly down the center of the empty road, the sound of his own footsteps echoing through the silent streets.

For the first time in his life, there were no lines to stand in, no delays to complain about, and no waiting for anything. There were no annoying coworkers, no screaming customers, no slow drivers cutting him off in traffic. No father to shout at him. No Glen to argue with.

There was nothing.

Ross wandered through the dead city in disbelief. Days may have passed. Or weeks. There was no way to tell anymore. The sky never changed. The streets never moved. The world had finally gotten out of his way. But as Ross looked across the endless, lifeless city, he realized there was no one left to share it with.

Suddenly, a woman's laughter echoed through the empty city. Ross lifted his head. In the distance, he caught a glimpse of a woman draped in tattered clothing, her lavender veil fluttering against her face.

It was her. The Siren of Pisces.

"Wait!" Ross shouted.

He stumbled after her, but his aged legs refused to keep pace. Every step grew heavier than the last, and the distance between them never seemed to shrink.

"Please!" Ross cried. "Take me from here! Let me go back!"

The woman only laughed again.

By the time Ross reached the place where he had seen her, she was gone.

Nothing remained except a trail of scattered red spots, leaving Ross alone in the endless silence.

THE END.

MEET THE AUTHOR

GetChrissy

GetChrissy loves to write. She enjoys using her quirky imagination to

create a world even more colorful than her own. When she is not working on her next adventure to share with her readers, you can find her practicing new skating tricks on her rollerblades.

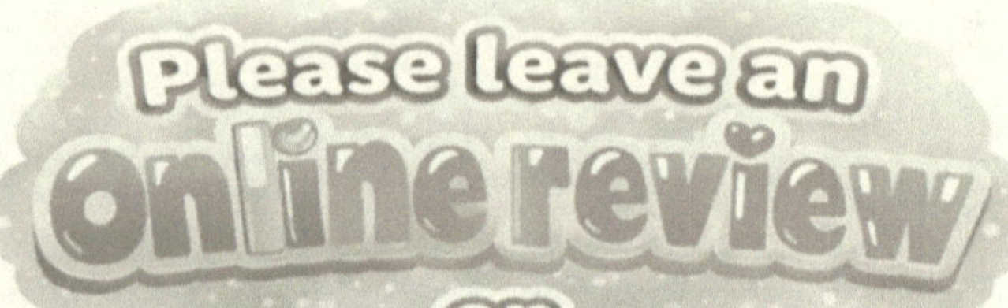

Amazon.com: Let's Fast Forward to the Good Stuff eBook : ., GetChrissy: Kindle Store

www.amazon.com

www.ingramcontent.com/pod-product-compliance
Lightning Source LLC
LaVergne TN
LVHW050934080826
845145LV00004B/1264

* 9 7 8 1 9 4 9 2 6 5 0 3 3 *